HIGH-WIRE COW

CLIVE SCRUTON

WITH WORDS BY DAVID LLOYD

WALKER BOOKS
LONDON

What's Cow reading now?

A good book.

I'll put on my crown

and my gown.

And now for a trick!

The high-heel kick!

Ha-ha! What a fall!

That's not all!

Race downhill and then—

watch out, Hen!

Become a high flier!

Hit the high wire!

Now spin and stand up!

Leg up! Hands up!

And to end the show

down we go!

What do you think?